CODENA QUICKSILVER

Sarah Dixon
Illustrated by Ann Johns

Designed by
Stephen Wright and David Gillingwater

Edited by Martin Oliver

Map illustrations by David Gillingwater
Additional designs by Ann Johns

Series Editor: Gaby Waters

Contents

About this Book

Codename Quicksilver is a thrilling adventure story, packed with fiendish codes and puzzles which must be solved to unravel the plot. Most of the puzzles are pretty difficult, so don't be surprised if you get stuck. There are clues on page 42 and you will find all the answers at the back of the book. If you don't need to look at these, you may well be a genius.

In Search of Quicksilver

HUDLUM CITY MAP

Sunnyside · Flipside · Upside · Seedyside · Ring Road

- Metro
- Tunnel
- Railway line
- Park
- Bridge

1 Galaxy Inc
2 Paragon Park Hotel
3 Paradise Hotel
4 Mercury Inc
5 Triangle Towers
6 Saturn Co
7 Avarice Heights
8 Grabbit Tower
9 Acme Aerosols
10 Olympian Heights
11 Star Enterprises
12 Mammon Mall
13 Planet Corp
14 Brief Encounters
15 Pagoda Club
16 The Fax
17 Tri-Advertizing Inc
18 Metropolis Club
19 Central Station
20 Pyramid Club
21 Hotel Glitz
22 Megabuck Towers
23 Hotel Luxuriance
24 Le Gourmet Rotunda
25 Gluttons

Mel checked her street map. She was somewhere in Seedyside, a part of Hudlum City she had never been to before. She was searching for a tape of Quicksilver's first album for her mother's birthday. As she looked around for helpful street signs, Mel noticed a grubby record shop on her left. Could it have the vital tape?

3

Kidnap!

Those early Quicksilver tapes are all the rage.

QUICKSILVER MEMORABILIA

LIME-GREEN PLATFORM BOOTS from Great Crashing Festival '75 – Orlando, Marmalade Grove, Strawberry Fields – 432-556
GOLD-PLATED PLECTRUM AND DRUM KIT – drums in need of repair – Macavity, Surf Shack (pink hut with blue steps), Blondi Beach – no phone
FUZZBOX, GUITAR LEADS AND FESTIVAL PHOTOS – Thomas Katz esq, 10 Jerry Buildings, Rattingdean – 555533
ORANGE AND GREEN CATSUIT from Los Spangles Festival '73 – Felix, Rough Ride Ranch, Sierra Bravada – no phone

Mel waited while the assistant searched the shelves. At last he reappeared, shaking his head. The shop had sold out of Quicksilver tapes. What could she do now? The assistant sifted through a stack of dusty magazines and pulled out a grubby copy of "Deadbeat Express".

"Try skimming through the small ads," he suggested. "You might find the tape you want for sale there."

Mel wandered out of the shop and down the backstreets, scanning the pages. Everything a Quicksilver fan could want was for sale – except the tape. She stuffed the magazine in her pocket and looked around.

She was lost. Ahead she saw a man slouching against a wall. Perhaps he might help . . . or perhaps not, she decided, glancing up at his sinister face.

Mel hurried along the street. Suddenly she heard footsteps running towards her. There was a loud CRASH behind her. She glanced nervously over her shoulder, then . . . THUD!

Mel came to, her head spinning. As she tried to sit up, a man pressed something into her hand.

Suddenly a car screeched to a halt, inches away from Mel. Its doors flew open. The man looked around frantically, then ran . . .

But he was too late. Two men pounced on him. They dragged him to the car and bundled him inside. Then one of them turned and gave Mel a chilling stare. She recognized him instantly.

"One word of this and you're dead meat," he snarled.

The door slammed shut and the car roared away. Mel staggered to her feet, dazed and confused. She looked down the street. The car had vanished. There was no sign that anything had happened, except . . . Mel opened her hand and straightened out a crumpled sheet of paper with numbers and letters scrawled on it. It looked like some kind of code. Could it be a secret message?

What does it say?

1 7 5 14 20 OCAHE
20 8 5 25 1 18 5 15 14 20 15
13 5 20 8 5 17 20 1 16 5 9
19 9 14 20 8 5 18 5 4 2 1
18 15 14 13 1 11 5 19 21
18 5 20 8 5 25 14 5 22 5
18 6 9 14 4 9 20 20 8 5 6
9 18 19 20 23 15 18 4 9 19
16 1 18 11 1 1 18 4 22 1 18 11

5

The Plot Thickens

W hat did the message mean? Mel's mind was buzzing with questions when she noticed something strange. There, on the pavement, were yellow marks, like the footprints of someone running very fast – like the man who had been bundled into the car.

Mel glanced anxiously over her shoulder, then followed the footprints down a dark alley. The trail ended at an overturned pot of paint. There was a dead end ahead. Where had the man come from? Mel jumped as a door banged open above her and swung in the wind.

She crept nervously up the fire escape and stepped inside. In the gloom below was a vast, derelict factory.

Holding her breath, Mel began to tiptoe along the metal walkway. Suddenly a shout shattered the silence. Mel froze . . .

"Turn round slowly," a stern voice ordered.

Mel tried to keep calm and did as she was commanded. Dreading what she might see, she looked up hesitantly. She gulped hard. A shadowy figure was reaching for his inside pocket . . .

"Luke Jones, special agent, Investigations Inc," he growled, flashing a tattered ID card. "Who are you? Why are you here?"

The agent's number jumped into focus. In a flash Mel remembered the coded message. She slowly reached into her pocket and handed over the crumpled piece of paper.

The agent groaned. He stumbled past Mel into a room, collapsed in a shabby armchair and stared miserably at the coded writing.

"What's going on?" Mel asked.

Agent 153185 didn't reply. Instead he sprang to his feet and seized an old flying trophy.

To Mel's astonishment, the agent unscrewed the base and fished out a Quicksilver cassette. She gaped in disbelief as he slotted it into a tape deck . . . then winced. Quicksilver sounded even worse than she remembered. The agent scowled, flicked the STOP button and impatiently unravelled the tape.

"It's not what I expected," he muttered, looking puzzled. "And it's covered with scratches."

But there was something odd about the scratches . . . and the badly handwritten index card.

"Perhaps it's a code," Mel said. "If I work out what it says, will you explain what's going on?"

The agent looked at Mel, thought hard, then finally nodded, "Okay, it's a deal."

Can you decipher the code?

Codename Quicksilver

Mel decoded the message, but it didn't make sense. Luke handed her the cassette for safe-keeping and led her out of the factory. Now it was his turn to tell her what was going on...

What I'm about to tell you is top-secret, but I hope I can trust you. It all began with three scientists, Dr Aardvark, Dr Bronsky and Professor "Mac" Macavity, working on a project codenamed Quicksilver, after Mac's favourite band.

Alone, late in the laboratory, Mac made an important scientific breakthrough – he created a volatile compound he called Q.

What sort of compound?

We don't know. Mac only told Aardvark and Bronsky, and all they've told us is that there could be terrible consequences if compound Q ends up in the wrong hands.

Before he was sentenced, Cortina made this secret gang salute to someone in the courtroom.

Theresa Green, Blondi Beach

The next week, Mac disappeared.

What happened to him?

Mac also left instructions for his colleagues. He sent a photo to Bronsky and a tape to Aardvark. Together, they reveal where the formula is hidden.

So this is the tape Mac sent to Dr Aardvark.

We don't know. But it seems he had written down the Q formula and concealed it at a secret location.

Yes. And it must be kept safe at all costs, because the week after Mac's disappearance, Bronsky and the photo vanished.

8

Gang Gala Night

Two hours later, Mel and Luke walked through the doors of the notorious Metropolis Club, haunt of hardened criminals and ruthless gangsters. The map message was their first lead. Now they knew that one of Aardvark's kidnappers would be in the club tonight.

"If you recognize anyone, give me a nod," Luke hissed. "Come on. Let's mingle."

Mel looked around doubtfully at the shady crowd.

"No, hang on, I've a better idea," Luke grinned. "We'll split up. I might recognize this Blade character from the I.I. crook files so I'll look for him and the instructions. Meet you by the exit at half past nine."

Feeling very out of place, Mel pushed her way to the bar. From there she could see everyone in the club – but what if she was recognized by the kidnapper? Mel shuddered and hastily grabbed a cocktail menu to hide her face.

It wasn't a cocktail menu. It was a seating plan for the Gang Gala Dinner. As she stared at the names, snatches of conversation drifted up from the dining tables below. In a flash, Mel realized she could identify Blade's seat. Now to grab the kidnapper's instructions . . .

Where is Blade's seat?

10

On the Trail of the Kidnappers

Al, I've got Chameleon's message. Jones has arrived with a meddling friend. I'll deal with the friend while you, Babs and Flash go ahead with the set-up as planned.

Fyhqdxq, -
Yikifusj qwudj
153185 ademi mxuhu jxu
jqfu yi. Xu mybb ru xuhu
jedywxj. Oek qdt Qb je iuj
jhqf. Tyiqffuqhqdsu je ru
unfbqydut ro Rqri' qdt
Vbqix'l YY isqd tqb vhqcu-
kf- ijeho yd jecehhem'i Vqn-
Sxqcubued

M el took a deep breath, ready to slip over to Blade's seat for the instructions, but a man beat her to it. Mel froze as she glimpsed his familiar, sinister face.

The man carefully extracted a slip of paper from the folds of a napkin. Mel watched as he collared a surly waiter and hissed some instructions. The waiter nodded and the man walked towards the exit.

There was no time to lose. Mel raced after the kidnapper. As he hurried outside, a small scrap of paper fluttered out of his jacket. Mel hardly had time to glance at it before stuffing it in her pocket.

The man disappeared down an alley and into a multi-storey car park. Mel tracked him as far as the third level, then lost sight of him. She crept behind a taxi and scanned the rows of cars. Was that a figure unlocking a car door? She inched forward to get a closer look . . .

Suddenly she was blinded by headlights. Strong arms grabbed her. A piece of rag was shoved in her face. Everything went black.

Meanwhile, back in the club, Luke was still searching for Blade and the instructions. At half past nine he glanced over to the exit. Where was Mel? His gaze fell on to the waiter at the table ahead. Why was he looking so shifty? Luke's thoughts were cut short as he crashed into a fat stranger.

Before Luke could apologize, the fat man beamed at him, shook hands and disappeared. Luke turned his attention back to the waiter. He was scribbling something on a menu. He glanced up surreptitiously, as if to make sure the coast was clear, then slipped the menu under a red placemat.

GANG GALA DINNER

Starters
Mplotov cocktail surprise
Last gazpacho
Giant krayfish
Grilled grapefruit

Main Courses
Joint of beef cased in a "cement overcoat"
Moll marnière
Chicken Cosa Nostra
Venison vendetta with squab

Roast racket of lamb with moonshine
Poached salmon- made to an old family recipe
Purloin steak
Sole survivor

Dessert
Crime caramel
Metropolis bombe surprise
Don's delight
Speakeasy soufflé
Godfather's gateau
Crêpes à la Casino Flambée

Four-Letter Block Codes
Messages are broken up into blocks of four letters, then the blocks and letters are rearranged in a variety of ways. Here are three popular ways of encoding the following sentence –

Rendezvous by the old bridge
Syndicate "N" Code
Igde lbdr teho ubsy
evzo rned
Patent Jemmie Code
Dner ovze ybsu oeht
rbdl egdi
Razor Muddle Code
Rned evzo ubsy teho
lbdr igde

As soon as the waiter disappeared behind the bar, Luke darted over to the table and grabbed the menu. He opened it and stared at . . . a list of dishes. But there were faint marks under some letters. Could it be yet another coded message?

Luke flipped through the cipher section of his I.I. Spy Fax to identify the code. There were three possibilities. But which was the right one?

What does the message say?

13

Eavesdropping

Mel opened her eyes and blinked. She was in a brightly-lit room. What had happened? Slowly she began to piece things together. The kidnap . . . the coded message . . . the Q tape . . . She dug in her pocket and pulled out a map, scraps of paper and a torn Deadbeat Express. The tape had gone. Her head still spinning, Mel staggered to the door and tugged at the handle.

The door was locked. But she could hear footsteps outside, heading her way. Someone was coming. What could they want? Mel didn't feel like finding out. She hid behind the door and waited . . . It swung open and in stomped the second kidnapper. Quick as a flash, Mel darted out behind him, slammed the door shut and rammed the bolts across.

Chameleon can't be with us tonight, but he left us this note sending his congratulations. Operation Quicksilver is going full steam ahead. Now we've got the tape and the photo, we don't need Aardvark.

We'll meet here at half past two tomorrow to divide the spoils.

Where was the tape?

We found it on a kid who saw the kidnap.

While the captive bellowed and hammered on the door, Mel sprinted up a flight of stairs into a long corridor. Suddenly a door opened behind her. Mel dived into a huge boardroom, wrenched open a cupboard and leapt inside. Her heart thudding, she peered out of a grill and watched a man march in. He scribbled a note, slapped it on the table and left.

Mel breathed a sigh of relief. She was just about to push the cupboard door open when the sinister kidnapper trooped into the room, followed by four shady strangers. Trapped in her cramped hiding place, Mel watched and listened hard. Who were these people? What was going on?

Who are they?

How shall we dispose of Aardvark?

I've decoded the message on the tape. I'll show you the results in a minute. Now we need the photo.

Chameleon left me the combination so I'll get it out of the safe.

I'll think about it. We've left him in the old ticket office at Grime Street Metro for the time being.

The kid's escaped! We've got to find her.

15

Secret Sequence

page 1

Piranha

Retunis of lsat mniteeg

Fniwollog fruliae to tcark dwon
Ktivacay, uuominans doisicen to
cgnahe paln. **Phnaria** and **Gepplrr** to
garb **Aravdrak** and tpae. **Cfia** to
ddocee **Kytivaca's** inoitcurtsns.
Bbas and **Fealh** to rveirtee flumroa
and pnalt Stacidnye ssirprue.

Tehn peecord wtih Ooitarepn
Qevliskciur as pennald. **Joe** to
bnirg beruhcors for our bugos
ctirahy, the SPS (Steicoy for
Poitcetorn of the Stacidnye) to
nxet mniteeg. **Ivy** to mkae
cnuopmod Q.

I.I. pnidivorg olarevl stirucey for
Mcubagek Trewos. **Gepplrr**, **Cnltroa**
and **Al** in pnoitisos V and W, and
Coelemahn in red hetpociler on
hapiled X (see paln of bnidliug) to
dael wtih cesirs. Bcnegremy sangil
- two tpas on red bepeelr bottun on
wiklae-tiklae.

page 2

At 2.00 **Joe** to aserdds coitnevnon
(in room mekrad Y - see paln of
bnidliug) on blahef of SPS wlihe
Ivy in cortnol room (Z) ppmus
cnuopmod Q tguorhh air-cninoitidnog
setsym. SPS (the Stacidnye) get
ltos of sevlir - qciuk!

Fniwollog ilbativene sseccus of
fnisiardnug, use cnuopmod Q to
sziee cortnol of crtnuoy - tehn
fllaniy the wlrod!

The room cleared instantly. Mel fell out of the cupboard, staggered to her feet and gulped. She was in the headquarters of the Syndicate, one of the three most ruthless gangs that stalked the city streets. And the Syndicate had the tape and the photo which would lead them to the secret Q formula. They had to be stopped, but how?

In a flash, Mel realized that the photo was still in the safe. If she found the photo, maybe she could beat the Syndicate to the formula.

Mel gave the dial on the safe an experimental twist. Immediately, a row of alarm lights began flashing. She snatched her hand away.

She had to find the combination fast. But where was it? As she looked around in desperation, Mel spotted the note that the sinister kidnapper had been holding. In their haste, the gang had left a vital clue.

What is the combination?

KING OF HEARTS

CIPHER OF THE DAY

AYDW EV XUQHTJ

CONVENTION OF THE CENTURY

The Fax - Friday 13th.

STRETCH LIMOS will line Megabuck Avenue as the world's richest people flock to Megabuck Towers for tomorrow's spectacular charity convention.

Glamorous former film star and owner of Megabuck Towers, Fay de Way, told the **FAX** that the convention will be held in the glitzy VRP Club for Very Rich People, right at the top of the Towers.

MYSTERY MAN

Mystery millionaire, "Casino" Joe will kick off the proceedings at two o'clock with a speech on behalf of a new charity, the SPS. "This SPS is a lot of new-fangled nonsense!" silent screen sweetheart, Greta Garble told the **FAX**.

"I hope everyone will give their money to my Donkeys in Distress."

BABS BALONEY, Chief Reporter

A vote at three o'clock will decide which lucky charity receives the millionaires' millions. Eccentric tennis ace, Ivor Lobb's Champions in Traction is the **FAX**'s hot favourite.

AMAZING DISCOVERY

Megabuck Towers

An Introduction
– with pull-out plan
by
Karl Bunkl
RIBENA

SPS £ ₣ ¥ $ £ DM ¥ ₣

Charity begins at home

Casino Joe, Chairman

Feeling hard-up? Lonely? Let the SPS take you by the hand and lead you to Norah and Gripper, fallen on hard times. The SPS cares about ordinary folk like Norah and Gripper. Dig deep into your pockets and give generously to the SPS. We'll make sure that all your donations go straight to Norah and Gripper and 11 other equally deserving cases.

Gripper, down on his luck

Norah, distressed gentry

Committee
L. Piranha, G.B. Hardman, B. Cortina, A. Terminator,
B. Baloney, F. Capone, M. Metropolis,
L. de Cifa, N. Kodar, A. Waits

Stowaway!

Six deft twists of the dial later, the safe door swung open. Mel reached right inside the safe until she found the photo. She shoved it in her pocket, then grabbed the playing card and the plan of Megabuck Towers from the table. She had a sneaking suspicion that they might prove useful.

Now Mel had to get out of the headquarters, fast. From every corner, alarm bells were clanging and sirens wailed.

Mel sprinted down the corridor, desperately looking for a way out. Suddenly she heard a yell. She had been spotted. There was a window ahead. Mel wrenched it open, took a deep breath and jumped . . .

Mel landed with a crunch in the yard below and dived into the back of an open van. She scrambled over a heap of cardboard boxes and hid behind a stack of crates.

More angry shouts rang out behind her. Mel froze as bright lights shone into the back of the van. But a long minute later, the lights snapped off and she was plunged back into darkness.

Mel sighed with relief. But she was not out of trouble yet. As she crawled out from her hiding place, the engine spluttered to life and the van lurched forwards.

The van rolled out of the HQ and turned right into the street. Mel could just make out a hoarse conversation. She shuddered as she caught the last, sinister words.

Hurry up, Gripper. You'll miss the rendezvous. We'll find that kid. No one ever escapes from the Syndicate alive.

Mel tried hard to memorize the van's route. As they accelerated, a train thundered overhead and in the distance she could hear the constant hum of the busy city.

The van shot through a red light, then screeched to a halt. A second set of traffic lights? While Gripper the driver revved the engine impatiently, Mel's mind clunked into gear. Now was her chance. She seized the door handle . . .

Suddenly the lights changed. Gripper stamped on the accelerator and veered sharply right. Mel went flying, along with boxes of frozen burgers, sauce bottles and buns.

Further on they swung right into a narrow street. Mel wiped a dollop of ketchup off her jacket and stared through the murky rear window at some shady characters lurking outside a warehouse.

Mel crossed her fingers, hoping they weren't going to stop in this seedy spot. She had seen enough gangsters for one day. Luckily Gripper seemed just as keen to keep going. With tyres squealing, he swerved left down a long, brightly-lit tunnel.

The van drove on through the seemingly endless tunnel. Mel gave up looking for landmarks and pulled out the photo she had taken from the safe. She held it up to the light and stared at the picture, and the writing below. For once it was a simple, uncoded message – or was it?

What is the message?

The Clique at large after graduation ceremony - Aardvark wearing his favourite wings from Red Baron Flying School - me before Vile Bodies gig - Bronsky recovering from unusually large quota of bean sprouts, mung beans, brown rice and chick peas.

Sewer Surprise

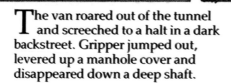

The van roared out of the tunnel and screeched to a halt in a dark backstreet. Gripper jumped out, levered up a manhole cover and disappeared down a deep shaft.

Mel decided to investigate. She climbed down after him into a long, dank, dripping tunnel. She could just make out his bulky shape in the murky gloom ahead. Further on, Gripper turned sharp left. Mel was plunged into pitch blackness. She blindly groped her way towards the turning, then . . .

SPLASH! Mel blundered into a foul-smelling stream of sludge. Gripper swivelled round.

"Come out!" he bellowed, beaming his torch along the dark tunnel. "It's no use hiding. I'll find you, wherever you are . . ."

Mel crouched in an old duct, hardly daring to breathe. Gripper walked slowly back down the passage towards her, playing his torch along the slimy walls. Any minute now, she would be discovered . . .

"Rats!" Gripper snorted.

Gripper turned and trudged on. When the coast was clear, Mel crawled out of the duct. Soaking wet and dripping with slime, she squelched after him. Gripper stopped at a junction, wedged a small package into the brickwork, then scurried down the left fork.

Mel was about to reach for the package, when she saw a flicker of light at the end of the right-hand tunnel. A dark figure crept towards her . . . It was Luke. She waved at him eagerly.

"Mel?" Luke gasped, goggle-eyed in disbelief. "What happened? How did you get here?"

"What about you?" she asked. "Why are you here? For a moment I thought you were a gangster."

"I'm following a great new lead," Luke explained. "According to a message I found in the Metropolis Club, the Razor Gang have left a package at this very junction."

"That's strange!" Mel exclaimed. "I've been following a member of the Syndicate through the sewers – and this is what he left."

She pulled Gripper's package out of its niche and thrust it in Luke's hands. They peered at its contents in the torchlight.

"Now we know where Aardvark is," Luke beamed.

"I'm not so sure," Mel frowned.

Where does Luke think Aardvark is? What does Mel think?

Jcak jion rnig raod aaïc maee rsoo lasn deha dosu ttha kfei rtsr ikgf tiun igno frfi nrgo akdu inoa Tenx rhTw etsb anud raod affi rtsj ucnt oTrh sotp affi rtsi omud rpoa adrv akro faft crav emro tleb Idae

New Toxin
Tiptown
Barewood
Little Eyre
Grayville
Blighton
Hudlum City
Smogsville
Coughin Town
Blottville
Fumesburg
Neucla Motel
Lake Effluence
High Lead

21

Subway Discovery

They surfaced in Upside, slimy, bedraggled and confused. How could Aardvark be in two different places? The map appeared to be from the Razor Gang, but had been delivered by a Syndicate man. Luke decided it was a joint operation, but Mel was sceptical. From what she had seen at the Syndicate's HQ, this looked like a one-gang show.

"The only solution is to check out both locations," Luke said, after several minutes' deep thought. "Let's try Grime Street Metro first. That's the nearest."

The station was right on the other side of the city. Luke waved his I.I. ID card and tried to hail a taxi, but with no success.

At last, footsore and weary, they reached Grime Street. The entrance to the disused station was just visible between shuttered shops. Luke hastily scrambled through a gap in the boarding and looked around. He was in a dimly-lit hall.

CRASH! With a flying kick, Luke opened the ticket office door and leapt inside.

"FREEZE!" he yelled. "Hands up!"

But the room was deserted.

Then they heard muffled cries coming from a locker in the corner.

"Stand back!" cried Luke.

He wrenched the door open and a familiar figure slowly toppled out. They had found Dr Aardvark.

"Luke, I never thought you'd find me," gasped Aardvark as they cut him free. "And your friend . . . you're the girl I gave the message to!"

"The Syndicate will be here soon with more threats," he continued once Mel had introduced herself. "They're determined to find the Q formula, but as long as my tape is safe, they'll never succeed."

His happy smile turned into a look of horror when Mel explained what had happened to the tape.

"But why does the Syndicate want the Q formula?" Luke asked.

"They're hatching a sinister plot," Aardvark replied. "I don't know the details but I have my suspicions. Compound Q is a hypnotic gas. When used incorrectly, it becomes a brainwashing agent."

Mel shivered. Quickly, she told the others what she had found out about Operation Quicksilver.

What is the Syndicate's plan?

Going Underground

Suddenly there was a crash outside. The Syndicate had arrived. Luke smashed open the Emergency Exit.

"Head for the tunnel," he cried.

With the Syndicate hot on their heels, the trio stumbled down to the deserted platform. They leapt inside an abandoned train, raced through the carriages, then jumped out into a tunnel. Angry shouts echoed behind them as they sprinted along the track to the next station.

"Now change lines," Luke panted, charging down an escalator.

Closely pursued by the crooks, they ran on through station after station, leaving puzzled cleaners in their wake.

They had to change lines three times to shake off the Syndicate thugs. As Gripper's yells faded away down a distant tunnel, the exhausted trio hurried on to a sixth station. They staggered up a flight of stairs and collapsed at the top.

"We've got to beat the gang to the formula," Mel gasped. "I found Mac's photo in their HQ – but the message doesn't make sense, and neither does the one on the tape."

"Knowing Mac, the messages are in some kind of double cipher," said Aardvark. "Read them together."

Minutes later, the real message was revealed. Now they knew where the Q formula was hidden, but they had to find the fastest route there. As a train rumbled beneath them, Mel had a brainwave. They could take the metro. She fished out a metro map that she had picked up in Grime Street ticket office. But it was years out of date and all the names of the lines were missing.

Where do they need to go?
What is their most direct route?

Peril in the Park

Twenty minutes later, the breathless trio charged up the escalator of Paragon Place Metro and ran out into Paragon Park. Now to find the Quicksilver statue.

In the centre of the park stood the Retsinian Deities, ancient statues from the ransacked Temple of Ironika. Luke barged past two early morning strollers and gaped at the nameplates of the statues, puzzled. Which one was Quicksilver?

"Try the statue of Mercury," Aardvark grinned. "Quicksilver is another name for mercury."

With his penknife at the ready, Luke dashed towards Mercury. The statue's nameplate was loose, so he frantically started tugging it free from the plinth. Suddenly Mel noticed the glint of a metal wire behind the nameplate . . .

"STOP!" she yelled.

Just in time, all three dived for cover as a deafening explosion ripped through the park.

Luke reached out and clutched . . . a dismembered arm! For a second, he panicked, then he realized it was stone. He looked around, dazed.

"The Syndicate has beaten us to the formula," gasped Mel, staggering to her feet. "How can we stop Operation Quicksilver now?"

"There's only one person who can put a halt to the gang's sinister schemes," Aardvark groaned. "And that's Mac. Before he disappeared, he was developing a Q neutralizer."

"If only we knew where the thugs are holding him," Luke sighed.

"But they haven't got Mac," cried Mel, remembering a coded document she had seen at the Syndicate's HQ. "Either another gang took him . . . or maybe he wasn't kidnapped at all."

She looked at the photo that she had found in the safe. Mac's face looked very familiar. She was sure she had seen him only yesterday.

Minutes later, Aardvark hailed a taxi. Everyone bundled inside. Now to reach Mac, fast.

Where is he?

27

To the Surf Shack

Luke was first out of the taxi. He hurried across to the heliport and flashed his I.I. ID card at the crew in the control tower.

"I want a helicopter to Blondi Beach," he ordered. "Now."

"Wait a minute," the chief controller replied, eyeing Luke's card suspiciously. "You'll need special clearance, even if you are an I.I. agent."

"Clearance can wait," Aardvark hissed as the controller turned away. "Follow me."

He grabbed Luke and Mel, propelled them out of the building and bundled them into the nearest helicopter. They gaped at the scientist, dumbstruck.

"I was the star pupil at the Red Baron School of Flying," Aardvark grinned as he seized the joystick.

Two hours later, the helicopter was hovering over Blondi Beach. Mel scanned the beach below for Mac's hideaway, the Surf Shack.

Minutes later, Aardvark landed outside a weather-beaten shack with peeling pink paint and grubby windows. Mel ran up the steps and hammered on its battered door.

There was no reply. Mel tried again . . . and again.

"Looks like no one's at home," Luke muttered, peering through a cracked, salt-sprayed windowpane.

They looked at each other glumly. They had flown all this way to find Mac and he wasn't even in.

Mel wandered over the dunes to the shore and watched surfers ride the huge rollers. A lone surfer sauntered back towards the shack. She stared at him . . .

"Professor Macavity?" she called. But the surfer kept on walking.

"The Syndicate's found the Q formula," Mel continued.

"Who are you?" hissed Mac, stopping dead in his tracks. "What do you know about the Q formula?"

Mac listened to Mel's story, but when he saw Luke sitting on the steps of the shack, he bristled.

"What are you doing with HIM?" he demanded. "Everyone knows about him and his gangster friends. It's all over today's newspaper."

It couldn't be true! For a second Mel gaped in disbelief at the paper lying by the step. Then everything fell into place. Luke had been framed – and she could prove it.

How?

The Fax

WIN A HOLIDAY TO MYTHIKA

IVOR LOBB – TENNIS RACKET REVELATIONS

FAX EXCLUSIVE

I.I. SCANDAL – AGENT LINK WITH GANG BOSS

BABS BALONEY, Chief Reporter

THE FAX can reveal that the youngest member of the world-famous secret agency, Investigations Inc, is working for the ruthless godfathers of the city's seedy underworld.

The **FAX** caught Jones red-handed, consorting with notorious gangland boss Jake the Toad at the Metropolis Club last night.

"We're best buddies, especially after the Prima Tua deal," laughed the Toad when the **FAX** rang him at his luxury penthouse flat. "He's also a close pal of Syndicate top gun, Baby Cortina."

HUDLUM JAILBREAK

Cortina is on the run, following his escape from Hudlum Island high security jail. Prison sources say that someone in the secret agencies must have been in the know. Was this someone Luke Jones? The **FAX** demands the FACTS.

Emergency Landing

Mac disappeared into his shack and emerged five seconds later, brandishing a canister of Q neutralizer. Everyone piled into the helicopter and soon Blondi Beach was a blur on the horizon.

Two hours later, they were flying over the city. Mel glanced at her watch. In half an hour, Operation Quicksilver would begin.

"We're running out of fuel fast," Aardvark gulped. "We'll have to land soon."

A red warning light flashed on the control panel as they hovered over Megabuck Towers.

"Where can I land?" Aardvark cried, gripping onto the joystick.

Suddenly the fuel gauge clicked to zero. The engine began to splutter ominously . . .

"WHERE?" screamed Aardvark.

Mel's brain sprang into action. She pulled out the Syndicate's plan of the skyscraper. They had to get to the control room, but only one landing pad led there. Could she find it in time?

Where can they land?

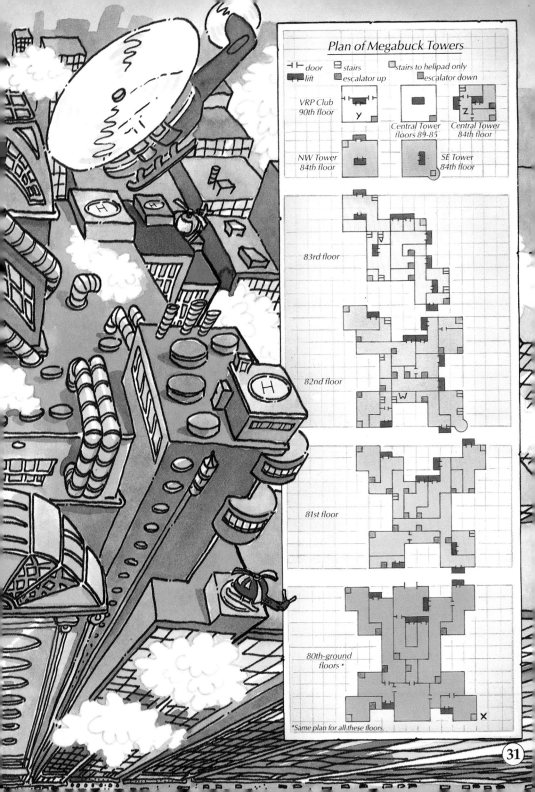

Plan of Megabuck Towers

⊢⊣ door ⌸ stairs ▧ stairs to helipad only
▨ lift ▧ escalator up ▧ escalator down

VRP Club 90th floor — Y

Central Tower floors 89-85

Central Tower 84th floor — Z

NW Tower 84th floor

SE Tower 84th floor

83rd floor — V

82nd floor — W

81st floor

80th-ground floors * — X

*Same plan for all these floors.

Into Megabuck Towers

Mel gaped out of the cockpit in horror as the helicopter spiralled downwards. At the last minute, Dr Aardvark wrenched the joystick up. The helicopter hovered in mid-air, then crash-landed on the south-east tower. Aardvark pulled the others out of the juddering wreck. They looked around, dazed.

"Th-th-that was a close shave," Luke stammered.

"Look out!" Aardvark yelled.

With a great CRACK, a rotor blade shot off the helicopter and whistled past Luke's left ear, missing it by inches.

Mel staggered to her feet and was nearly blown off the edge of the tower by a sudden gust of wind.

"Get to the door!" Mac ordered, grabbing hold of her. "Three narrow escapes are enough for one day."

With a roar, the wind smashed against the helicopter, ripping away the remaining rotors and shattering the windows. Lethal fragments cut through the air as the four dashed across the roof. Up ahead, Luke tried to radio through to the I.I. agents providing security for the convention, but all he could get was static.

At last they reached the door – but it was locked. How could they get in? Luke stared blankly at the keys on the entry panel. Then he remembered. Quickly, he punched in his agent and organization numbers in I.I. code. The door clicked open and everyone dived inside Megabuck Towers.

Clutching the plan tightly, Mel led the way to the control room. They whizzed between floors in lifts, charged down escalators, puffed and panted up stairs, and finally piled into a service lift.

The lift stopped with a jolt right outside the control room. But its doors remained firmly shut. A message flickered across a small screen in front of them, "Enter Access Number".

Luke keyed in his agent number. Nothing happened. He tried putting his number into every code he knew, but it was hopeless.

"Is there a special security sequence for the day?" Mel asked. "Would I.I. HQ have it?"

Luke anxiously radioed through. The four listened to HQ's reply with bated breath . . .

Mel's heart sank. Any minute now, Operation Quicksilver would begin . . . and succeed, all because they were trapped in a lift.

They would never work out the secret sequence to open the lift door. The information from HQ was useless – or was it?

What is the sequence?

Control Room Crisis

Everyone held their breath as Mac tapped in the secret sequence. Only the lift door separated them from a ruthless Syndicate villain.

Suddenly the lift door slid open. They stared into the control room. Mac and Aardvark gasped . . .

Dr Bronsky! Their missing colleague was crouching over a large air-conditioning vent, armed with a gleaming metallic cylinder of Q gas. So she had been a member of the sinister gang all the time.

"STOP!" Mac bellowed.

Dr Bronsky spun round and released a jet of Q gas straight at him. Mac ducked just in time. Quickly, Mel grabbed the canister of Q neutralizer from Mac and pressed the trigger. There was a long HISS of escaping gas.

"Compound Q is harmless now," Mel grinned. "I've neutralized it. Operation Quicksilver has failed."

Luke, Mac and Aardvark leapt out of the lift and tied Bronsky up. The evil scientist sneered at them.

"You may have caught me, but you're too late!" she smirked. "I've already contaminated the air-conditioning system with Q."

"Hurry!" Mac cried. "Pump the neutralizer up the vent."

"You'll need to switch on the system first," Bronsky laughed.

"Where's the ON button?" squawked Luke, pointing at hundreds of controls.

Bronsky watched with glee as the four jabbed buttons, twisted dials and pulled levers, throwing every system into overdrive – except the air-conditioning system.

Where WAS the button? Mel looked around desperately. Out of the corner of her eye, through a haze of steam and flashing lights, she saw Bronsky's foot tap twice against a small walkie-talkie.

"That's the Syndicate distress signal," Bronsky purred. "My friends are coming to get you. There's no escape."

As if on cue, the lift began to open and footsteps thundered down a nearby passage. Mel kept cool. She knew Bronsky was wrong. There was an escape route – and a few vital seconds left to find the ON button.

Where is the escape route?

Chaos

Just before Bronsky's sidekicks burst in, Luke punched a small red button. With a great whoosh, the neutralizer was sucked through the system. As the four ran out of the room, Mac grabbed Bronsky's case.

"Take this to I.I. HQ," he hissed to Luke. "The Q formula's inside."

They raced down to the 82nd floor, took a wrong turning up an escalator and jumped into a huge gilt lift. It zoomed upwards.

To their surprise, they stepped out of the lift into the VRP Club. Mel blinked, dazzled by sparkling chandeliers. A fat, cigar-wielding man was addressing the convention. He was Casino Joe of the Syndicate and he was just finishing his phony spiel.

" . . . and that's why you must give all your money to the SPS," he smiled. "Hands up if you agree."

Had the neutralizer reached the club in time? Mel watched Casino Joe's audience anxiously . . .

"Hold on," yelled a woman. "What about Donkeys in Distress?"

At once, everyone began shouting. Casino Joe's smile turned into a snarl. He glanced at the lift and caught Mel's look of triumph.

Just then the lift doors opened behind Mel. Gripper, Al and Cortina leapt out, disguised as security guards. The VRPs dived for cover, scattering files and papers, as Luke vaulted across the conference table and raced for the escalator, clutching the case. Casino Joe and his cronies charged after him.

"We'll take care of this one!" Joe cried to a huddle of I.I. agents in the corner. "You get the rest!"

The agents promptly pounced on Mel, Mac and Aardvark.

"You're making a BIG mistake," Mel shouted, struggling to break free from the agents. "The real villains are getting away."

As Gripper swung past on a chandelier and disappeared after Luke, Mel tried to explain about Operation Quicksilver and the Syndicate to the sceptical agents.

"You MUST believe me," she insisted. "We've left one of them tied up in the control room."

"You'd better be right," an agent muttered, then took out his radio. "Put all staff on red alert . . ."

Mel's watch bleeped 2.30. In a flash she realized that they could round up the rest of the gang at their secret meeting . . . if only she could remember where their HQ was.

Where is the Syndicate's HQ?

No Escape?

With Casino Joe, Cortina, Gripper and Al hard on his heels, Luke zigzagged through the upper floors of Megabuck Towers, desperately clinging on to Mac's case.

By the 81st floor, the Syndicate crooks were still on his trail. If only he could shake them off. Quickly, Luke leapt into the first lift he saw and jabbed the down button. With alarming speed, the lift plunged hundreds of feet into the glass foyer below. Luke waited for his stomach to catch up with him, then dashed to the entrance.

"There's no escape," a voice growled. "Hand over the case."

The four Syndicate heavies barred his escape. Luke gritted his teeth and swung the case through the glass wall.

He clambered through the jagged hole onto the pavement and dodged past bewildered tourists.

"You haven't seen the last of us yet!" Gripper bellowed behind him.

Cars squealed to a halt, horns blaring angrily, as Luke darted across the road to the river. On the opposite bank, he could just make out the I.I.'s HQ – and safety.

Gasping for breath, Luke raced along the endless embankment. At last he reached a bridge. Close to exhaustion, he stumbled across.

Suddenly a car swerved in front of him. Cortina and Casino Joe jumped out. Al and Gripper were catching him up. He was trapped, unless . . .

Blood pounding in his ears, Luke hoisted himself on to the girders of the bridge and began to climb. The case grew heavier and heavier...

At the top Luke clung to a metal support. He could go no further. A helicopter whirred above him. Help at last. A rope ladder dropped from the hatch and a man with a megaphone leaned out. Luke smiled, relieved, as he recognized the friendly face of the I.I. captain.

"You can hand the case to me now!" the captain shouted.

As Luke held out the case, a car zoomed on to the bridge, sending the crowds surging back, and screeched to a halt. Suddenly he heard a high-pitched voice above the commotion...

"Don't do it!" Mel yelled.

Why not?

River Rendezvous

With a snarl, the captain lunged for the case. But Luke was not going to let him or the Syndicate heavies have it. Taking a deep breath, he dived into the depths of the murky river below.

Luke surfaced spluttering, but still clutching the vital case. A speedboat carefully drew up beside him and Aardvark threw him a rope.

Dripping and bewildered, Luke clambered aboard. Over his shoulder, he watched as detectives dragged the furious I.I. captain from his helicopter.

"What's going on?" he asked.

"The Syndicate's been smashed," Mel explained. "All 13 members have been captured, including the gang's ruthless leader, Chameleon, alias the I.I.'s double-crossing captain."

"Operation Quicksilver has been a total failure," laughed Aardvark.

"Have you got my case?" Mac asked. "Is the Q formula safe?"

Luke proudly handed over the case. Then, with a sinking feeling, he noticed that the clasps were broken. Mac gaped inside, horrorstruck.

"It must have fallen out," Luke mumbled. "Why is it so important? We've got the neutralizer."

"We don't want the Q formula to fall into the wrong hands again," gulped Mac. "We might not be able to foil another sinister plot in time."

"Don't panic," Aardvark grinned. "I know where the formula is."

Where is it?

40

SINISTER SYNDICATE PLOT FOILED

ROSY PARKER,
Chief Reporter

THE SYNDICATE, one of the three ruthless gangs that rule the city's seedy underworld has been BUSTED. Their fiendish plot to seize control of the world has been foiled, thanks to plucky Mel Lee and junior secret agent Luke Jones.

In the first stage of the gang's sinister plan, Syndicate member and gambling king Casino Joe posed as a bogus charity boss and tried to con millions from multi-millionaires at the VRP charity convention.

But Mel and Luke scotched Casino's crooked scheme. In a dramatic chase, Casino and his cronies were rounded up at Rusty Gate Suspension Bridge. The rest of the Syndicate were picked up at a secret meeting in the gang's penthouse HQ off Avarice Avenue.

SYNDICATE SHOCK

Last night, in an exclusive FAX interview, Mel Lee revealed that the Syndicate's mystery boss and criminal mastermind, I.I. CAPTAIN JOHN SILVER.

"I can't believe it," stunned silver-haired I.I. receptionist, Beryl Twinset told the FAX. "He was such a nice man."

Syndicate members include a leading banker, an accountant, a top spy, a reporter and a missing scientist working on a top-secret project codenamed Quicksilver.

RIVAL GANGS' GLEE

AS ALL 13 MEMBERS of the Syndicate cooled their heels in Hudlum Island High Security Jail last night, rival gangsters from the Jemmies and Razor Gang celebrated at Blade's Bar (formerly the Metropolis Club).

"We're delighted at the news," a relieved Ronnie Razor told the FAX. "The Syndicate broke the Skid Row Pact, then tried to frame us and the Jemmies for everything they did. Good riddance!"

COVER-UP?

One question remains. HOW did the Syndicate intend to achieve their final aim of world domination? Is there a COVER-UP? The FAX demands the FACTS.

Friday 27th

DIVING DISCOVERY

Former secret agent and new Olympic hopeful, Luke Jones, sponsored by the FAX. Pics of Jones's dramatic diving debut in full on p.3.

Sunday 15th

AMAZING VRP CHARITY DECISION

AFTER a dramatic beginning, the glitzy VRP Charity Convention reached an astonishing climax. Glamorous former film star and owner of Megabuck Towers, Fay de Way announced that multi-millionaires voted to give their millions to ALL the charities.

"Every charity will benefit," explained Donkeys in Distress president Greta Garble. "Except that bogus Syndicate outfit, the SPS!"

Last night Fay de Way told the FAX she is turning Megabuck Towers into a fabulous THEME PARK.

PARTY TIME

The building will be full of AMAZING MAZES and FUN RIDES – and it will all be FREE. Before the builders move in, there will be a huge party. EVERYONE in the city is invited.

Surf Shack
Blondi Beach

Dear Mel,
Here's that Quicksilver tape you were looking for.
Happy listening! Drum kit?
...len plectr...
...mer Aard...
...Shack?
...ng Qu...
Love
Mac

12c Arcadian Ave
Sunnybrook
Spring County

Dear Mac,
Thanks for the tape. Mum's over the moon and plays it all the time. I've just bought myself some earplugs!
Can't wait to see you, Dr Aardvark and the Olympic hopeful at Blondi Beach next summer.
Love Mel X

Clues

Pages 4-5

Try substituting letters for numbers and numbers for letters.

Pages 6-7

Line up the scratches with the letters below and try reading downwards. Remember the previous message. Don't worry if your solution doesn't make sense.

Pages 8-9

Try rearranging the letters between the first and last letter of each word. Can you match the symbols with those on the map on page 3?

Pages 10-11

Solve this by a process of elimination. Which tables can you rule out? You don't need to work out where everyone sits.

Pages 12-13

Read the letters above the dots, then try applying the codes in Luke's Spy Fax.

Pages 14-15

Has the sinister kidnapper mentioned any of his associates? Look at the woman with grey hair.

Pages 16-17

Look at the playing card for the cipher. How can KING OF HEARTS become AYDW EV XUQHJI?

Pages 18-19

Have you spotted the dots? Don't worry if your solution doesn't make sense.

Pages 20-21

Do you recognize this code? Is the map the right way round? And what did Mel overhear at the secret meeting?

Pages 22-23

Read the coded minutes on page 16. They are in a familiar code.

Pages 24-25

This is tricky. Reverse the order of the words in each message and try combining them to make a sentence. You may have to crack the code by trial and error. Before you can work out where the trio must go, you have to find out where they are. Look at the names of the lines and the order in which they appear. Remember they have changed lines three times and have reached their sixth station.

Pages 26-27

Look back. Remember Mac's full name.

Pages 28-29

Try decoding the message dropped by the sinister kidnapper on page 12. Use the playing card cipher.

Pages 30-31

Look at the coded minutes on page 16. This is a three-dimensional maze.

Pages 32-33

This is easy.

Pages 34-35

Where are the gangsters positioned?

Pages 36-37

Look back to Mel's journey on pages 18 and 19. Can you match up the route with the map on page 3? Can you find the name of the street? Try comparing the map on page 3 with the metro map on page 25.

Pages 38-39

Do you recognize the helicopter? Have you seen this man before?

Page 40

Look back and use your eyes.

Answers

Pages 4-5

The numbers represent letters and the letters represent words, so that 1=A and A=1, 2=B and B=2, and so on to the end of the alphabet. With punctuation and spaces added, the decoded message says:

AGENT 15 3 18 5 – THEY ARE ON TO ME. THE Q TAPE IS IN THE RED BARON. MAKE SURE THEY NEVER FIND IT. THE FIRST WORD IS PARK. – AARDVARK

Pages 6-7

Mel uses the scratches on the tape to decipher the code. First she positions the tape above the first line, placing the first scratch above the letter P. Then she reads down the column of letters below the scratch. This produces the word PARK. Mel reveals the rest of the message by reading down the columns below the other scratches. The complete message is:

PARK IN STATUE NAMEPLATE HIDDEN IS

This may not make sense but Mel is sure she has decoded the message correctly because the coded message on page 5 told her "the first word is park".

Pages 8-9

The letters between the first and last letters of each word on the intercepted message are written in reverse order. The first and last letters remain the same. Decoded, the message says:

CHAMELEON – GRIPPER AND I PICKED UP AARDVARK BUT WE COULD NOT FIND THE Q TAPE. SEND FURTHER INSTRUCTIONS TO BUILDING MARKED X ON MAP. LEAVE THEM UNDER NAPKIN AT BLADE'S SEAT. I WILL COLLECT THEM AT NINE – PIRANHA

The symbols below the message match some of those on the city map. This suggests that they are a map of some sort. If you superimpose them on Mel's map of Hudlum City, you can see that X marks the position of building 18, the Metropolis Club.

The matching symbols are marked in green.

HUDLUM CITY MAP

- Metro
- Tunnel
- Railway line
- Park
- Bridge

1 Galaxy Inc
2 Paragon Park Hotel
3 Paradise Hotel
4 Mercury Inc
5 Triangle Towers
6 Saturn Co
7 Avarice Heights
8 Grabbit Tower
9 Acme Aerosols
10 Olympian Heights
11 Star Enterprises
12 Mammon Mall
13 Planet Corp
14 Brief Encounters
15 Pagoda Club
16 The Fax
17 Tri-Advertizing Inc
18 Metropolis Club
19 Central Station
20 Pyramid Club
21 Hotel Glitz
22 Megabuck Towers
23 Hotel Luxuriance
24 Le Gourmet Rotunda
25 Gluttons

Mel can locate Blade's seat by a process of elimination. She correctly assumes that the people at the dining tables are sitting in their places and she knows that Blade has not arrived yet, because the woman in green at table A says so. It is also clear from what she is saying that Blade will sit at another table, so Mel can rule out the empty seat at table A.

According to the thin waiter speaking to Mr Metropolis, no members of rival gangs are sitting at the same table.

With the aid of the seating plan and snippets of conversation, Mel can identify the man at table B as Goldfingers Loot of the Jemmies and the woman at table D as Babs Baloney of the Syndicate. As Blade is a member of the Razor Gang, he cannot sit at either table.

Mel can also identify the man at the table in the bar area to her left as Officer Carver of the Razor Gang. He will be sitting right behind Krystal the singer. The only seats left that allow him to do this are at tables B and E. He will be sitting at E.

But Blade cannot sit in the seat opposite Officer Carver on table E, as the woman in green at table A says he will be sitting right opposite a car dealer.

This leaves table C. As Blade cannot be sitting opposite the man addressed as councillor, he is left with the seat opposite the man in the white hat, who must be the car dealer.

To decipher the message, Luke first reads the letters above the dots then divides them into blocks of four, as instructed by his I.I. Spy Fax. This is the result:

TKAE PCAK AEGT OUJN CITO NINN ENIS EEWR STAT WAOM ADNL EVAE IUNS ULAP LCAE

By a process of elimination, Luke works out that the message is in Razor Muddle Code. When he follows the instructions in his Spy Fax, this message is revealed:

TAKE PACKAGE TO JUNCTION NINE IN SEWERS AT TWO AM AND LEAVE IN USUAL PLACE.

According to Luke, Aardvark's kidnap is the work of either the Syndicate, the Jemmies or the Razor Gang. As the gangs have fallen out and broken the Skid Row Pact after a shootout on Seedyside (pages 3 and 9), it is unlikely that more than one gang is involved in the kidnap.

In the intercepted message on page 9, one of the kidnappers arranges to pick up further instructions under a napkin at Blade's seat in the Metropolis Club. Mel knows from the seating plan on page 11 that Blade is a member of the Razor Gang. This suggests that Blade might be involved and that the kidnap is the work of the Razor Gang.

But after Piranha, the sinister kidnapper, picks up the instructions, Mel overhears him tell the large waiter on page 12 "You, Babs and Flash go ahead with the set-up as planned". He is obviously referring to Babs Baloney and Flash Capone who are listed on the seating plan as members of the Syndicate. This seems to suggest that Aardvark's kidnap was a Syndicate operation. Mel finds this very confusing.

At the secret meeting, Mel rules out the Razor Gang in face of strong evidence pointing to the Syndicate. She decides Blade was not involved in the kidnap and his seat was just used as a message drop.

Pages 14-15 (continued)

When the grey-haired woman enters the room, she makes a secret signal which Mel recognizes instantly. It is the secret Syndicate gang salute, which Mel saw on television (page 8) during a news report on Baby Cortina, the escaped Syndicate gangster. If you flip back to the Metropolis Club, you can see other members of the gang using this secret signal.

Pages 16-17

Mel spots the playing card with CIPHER OF THE DAY written on it. She notices that the strange words AYDW EV XUQHJI on the bottom of the card have the same number of letters in the same grouping as the words KING OF HEARTS on the top of the card. Mel realizes that AYDW EV XUQHJI is KING OF HEARTS written in a shifted alphabet code which starts with K and ends with J so that K=A, L=B, M=C and so on. The note on yellow paper is written in the same alphabet. Decoded, it says:

PIRANHA, CONGRATULATIONS ON THE GOOD WORK. UNABLE TO STAY FOR MEETING. PHOTO IN SAFE. COMBINATION – USUAL SIX-NUMBER SEQUENCE STARTING WITH FIVE. CHAMELEON

Assuming that a sequence is a regular pattern of numbers, there is only one possible six-number sequence on the dial. It is 5 7 11 17 25 35. The jump between the numbers increases by two each time.

Pages 18-19

Mel spots faint dots below some of the letters which reveal this incomprehensible message:

QALUMROFDNIHEBFOREVLISKCIUQNO GARAP

When this message is read backwards and spaces are added, it forms these words:

PARAGON QUICKSILVER OF BEHIND FORMULA Q

They do not make sense, but neither did Mac's previous message on the Q tape.

Pages 20-21

Like the message on page 13, this message is in Razor Muddle Code. Decoded, it says:

JACK, JOIN RING ROAD AT ACME AEROSOLS AND HEAD SOUTH. TAKE FIRST RIGHT TURNING OFF RING ROAD. TURN ONTO NORTHWEST BOUND ROAD AT FIRST JUNCTION. AT NEXT JUNCTION TAKE ROAD HEADING DUE NORTH. STOP AT FIRST TOWN. DROP AARDVARK OFF AT CARVER MOTEL. BLADE

The blue road on this map is the ring road. When Luke compares the postions of the turnings off the ring road with those on Mel's map on page 3, he realizes that this map is the wrong way round and that north is pointing to the bottom left-hand corner. Now it is easy to follow the directions. The route is marked in black and it leads to Fumesburg.

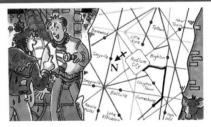

Mel cannot believe that Aardvark is at Fumesburg. At the secret meeting on page 14 she overheard Piranha, the sinister kidnapper, say that Aardvark was in the old ticket office at Grime Street Metro. She is very confused. From what she has seen, this is a Syndicate operation. But she cannot understand why the Syndicate man, Gripper, left a Razor Gang message. She wonders whether this might be a false trail laid by the Syndicate to make Luke think it is the work of the Razor Gang.

While Mel was searching for the safe's combination on page 16, she read the newspaper cutting about the Charity Convention and the coded minutes. This is what the minutes say:

Minutes of last meeting

Following failure to track down **Macavity**, unanimous decision to change plan. **Piranha** and **Gripper** to grab **Aardvark** and tape. **Cifa** to decode **Macavity's** instructions. **Babs** and **Flash** to retrieve formula and plant Syndicate surprise.

Then proceed with Operation Quicksilver as planned. Joe to bring brochures for our bogus charity, the SPS (Society for Protection of the Syndicate) to next meeting. **Ivy** to make compound Q.

I.I. providing overall security for Megabuck Towers. **Gripper**, **Cortina** and **Al** in positions V and W, and **Chameleon** in red helicopter on helipad X (see plan of building) to deal with crises. Emergency signal – two taps on red bleeper button on walkie-talkie.

At 2.00 **Joe** to address convention (in room marked Y – see plan of building) on behalf of the SPS while **Ivy** in control room (Z) pumps compound Q through air-conditioning system. SPS (the Syndicate) get lots of silver – quick!

Following inevitable success of fundraising, use compound Q to seize control of country – then finally the world!

Now that Aardvark has explained that compound Q is a hypnotic gas which can be used as a brainwashing agent, Mel instantly realizes what the gang's fiendish plan is. They intend to use compound Q to brainwash the millionaires at the Megabuck Towers Charity Convention into handing all their money to the SPS, a bogus charity run by the Syndicate for their own benefit. Then the evil gang will use compound Q to take over the country, and then the world.

First of all, they have to find the hiding place of the Q formula. To crack Mac's double cipher, they must put the two messages together. This is tricky as there is no obvious way of combining the messages. After a process of trial and error, they reverse the order of the words in each part of the message. The first message now says:

IS HIDDEN NAMEPLATE STATUE IN PARK

The second message now says:

Q FORMULA BEHIND OF QUICKSILVER PARAGON

Then they take two words from the second message, then two from the first, then one from the second and one from the first, then two words from each message again, then one from each. This reveals the final message:

Q FORMULA IS HIDDEN BEHIND NAMEPLATE OF QUICKSILVER STATUE IN PARAGON PARK.

To find the most direct route to Paragon Park, they must first work out where they are. Since they left Grime Street, they have changed lines three times to reach the sixth station. When they remember the names of the lines in some of the stations they have run through, they realize there is only one route that they could have taken. It leads to Hotel Glitz.

After matching up the placenames and positions of the metro stations on the metro map with Mel's map of Hudlum City, they can see that Paragon Place is the nearest station to Paragon Park.

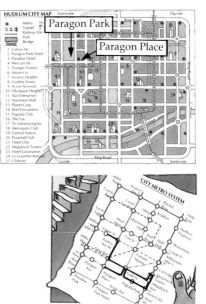

Their route from Grime Street to Paragon Park via Hotel Glitz is marked in black.

Pages 26-27

Mel has seen Mac's face before, on a television screen on page 8. The location, Blondi Beach, reminds her of an advert in the Quicksilver Memorabilia section of Deadbeat Express (page 4) – Macavity, Surf Shack, Blondi Beach. Mel knows that Mac's full name is Professor Macavity and remembers Luke telling her that Mac was a Quicksilver fan, so she realizes that this must be Mac's address.

Theresa Green, Blondi Beach

Pages 28-29

In her pocket, Mel has a message on pink paper, dropped by Piranha, the sinister kidnapper, on page 12. Now she has the playing card with the cipher of the day, she realizes the message on the pink paper is in the same code as the note on yellow paper (page 17). Decoded, the message provides her with proof that Luke has been framed. This is what it says:

PIRANHA – I SUSPECT AGENT 153185 KNOWS WHERE THE TAPE IS. HE WILL BE HERE TONIGHT. YOU AND AL TO SET TRAP. DISAPPEARANCE TO BE EXPLAINED BY BABS' AND FLASH'S I.I. SCANDAL FRAME-UP STORY IN TOMORROW'S FAX – CHAMELEON

Pages 30-31

From the coded minutes on page 16, Mel knows they will find a member of the Syndicate called Ivy with compound Q in the control room marked Z. To get there, they should land on the helipad on the south-east tower and follow the route marked in black.

They should land here. ———

Plan of Megabuck Towers

door · stairs · stairs to helipad only
lift · use escalator up · use escalator down

VRP Club
90th floor

Central Tower
floors 89-85

Central Tower
84th floor

NW Tower
84th floor

SE Tower
84th floor

83rd floor

82nd floor

81st floor

80th-ground
floors*

*Same plan for all these floors

Door on east wall.

Pages 32-33

This sequence proved to be surprisingly simple. It is 4 6 5 7 6 8 7 9. The jumps between the numbers increase by two, then decrease by one, then increase by two again and increase by one, and so on.

Pages 34-35

Their escape route from the control room is through the door on the east wall. This route avoids the Syndicate gangsters who have run from positions V and W in response to Bronsky's emergency signal and are about to enter the control room via the lift and the door on the north wall.

Their escape route is marked in red on the plan above.

Pages 36-37

The Syndicate's secret HQ is at 13 Avarice Avenue.

Mel works this out by remembering the route taken by Gripper's van from the HQ on pages 18 and 19. She matches up this route and the landmarks she saw through the van's rear window with her map of the city. The route is marked in red.

To find out the name of the street where the Syndicate's HQ is located, Mel compares the positions of the metro stations on her map of the city with those on the metro map (page 25). From this she realizes that the HQ is on Avarice Avenue. Fortunately she was able to spot the number – 13, unlucky for some!

Here is the view looking west from this junction

Railway bridge

First right turn

Second right turn

Left turn down the tunnel

Avarice Ave W Metro   Avarice Ave E Metro

Pages 38-39

The I.I. captain is none other than Chameleon, the shadowy leader of the Syndicate. Thinking back to the coded minutes and the plan of Megabuck Towers, Mel knows that Chameleon is in the red helicopter in the position marked X. When they are hovering over the skyscraper on page 31, she can see Chameleon's helicopter below. The I.I. captain is flying an identical red helicopter. Even its number is the same.

More important still, Mel has seen the I.I. captain before – in the Syndicate HQ on page 15. She watched him write a note which she later decoded to find the safe combination. The note was signed "Chameleon".

Geniuses and serious decoders might have had their suspicions about the I.I. captain before now. If Luke's agent and organization numbers are encoded to make the words OCAHE LEON on page 32, what word do the I.I. captain's agent and organization numbers form using the same code?

Page 40

The vital Q formula fell out of the case in the lift that Luke jumped into on the 81st floor (page 38). Luckily the Syndicate thugs were in the other lift, so they did not pick it up. Fortunately Aardvark spotted it lying on the floor when he, Mel and Mac were finding their way out of Megabuck Towers.

First published in 1991 by
Usborne Publishing Ltd,
Usborne House,
83-85 Saffron Hill,
London EC1N 8RT, England

Copyright © 1991 Usborne Publishing Ltd.

The name Usborne and the device 🎈 are Trade Marks of Usborne Publishing Ltd.

Printed in Italy